THE TERRANS COOK UP
SOME MISCHIEF!

By Ryder Windham

Illustrated by Patrick Spaziante

Simon Spotlight

New York   London   Toronto   Sydney   New Delhi

This book is a work of fiction. Any references to historical events, real people, or real places are used fictitiously. Other names, characters, places, and events are products of the author's imagination, and any resemblance to actual events or places or persons, living or dead, is entirely coincidental.

SIMON SPOTLIGHT

An imprint of Simon & Schuster Children's Publishing Division
1230 Avenue of the Americas, New York, New York 10020
This Simon Spotlight edition August 2023
TRANSFORMERS and all related characters are trademarks of Hasbro and are used with permission. TRANSFORMERS © 2023 Hasbro. All Rights Reserved. Transformers: EarthSpark TV series © 2023 Hasbro/Viacom International Inc. All Rights Reserved. Nickelodeon is a trademark of Viacom International Inc. All rights reserved, including the right of reproduction in whole or in part in any form. SIMON SPOTLIGHT and colophon are registered trademarks of Simon & Schuster, Inc. For information about special discounts for bulk purchases, please contact Simon & Schuster Special Sales at 1-866-506-1949 or business@simonandschuster.com.
Designed by Brittany Fetcho
The illustrations for this book were rendered digitally.
The text of this book was set in Proxima Nova.
Manufactured in the United States of America 0723 OFF
10 9 8 7 6 5 4 3 2 1
ISBN 978-1-6659-4016-0 (hc)
ISBN 978-1-6659-4015-3 (pbk)
ISBN 978-1-6659-4017-7 (ebook)

CONTENTS

CHAPTER 1
A SEAT AT THE TABLE

Bumblebee was watching Twitch, Thrash, Hashtag, Nightshade, and Jawbreaker playing tag outside the barn on the Malto family farm when Thrash said, "Everybody freeze!"

All five Terrans stopped suddenly. Bumblebee said, "What's wrong?"

Thrash said, "This game would be more fun if Mo and Robby joined in."

Nightshade said, "I believe they are

still partaking in their evening meal."

"It's too bad we don't eat food," Twitch said. "Then we could join them."

"But we're family too," Thrash said. "We should be with them, even if we don't eat!"

"Let's see if they're finished," Hashtag said.

Leaving Bumblebee at the barn, the Terrans marched over to the Malto family's house. Looking through the kitchen's wide-open windows, they saw Dot Malto seated at a table with Mo and Robby. Twitch said, "Hey, Mom, is dinner over yet?"

"Not quite," Dot said. "Dad is getting the—"

"Dessert!" Alex Malto said as he carried a large purple cake to the table. "My mother's recipe for *ube-macapuno* cake will satisfy the biggest sweet tooth!"

"Good to know," Mo said, "because my sweet tooth is enormous!"

As Alex placed the cake on the table, Thrash leaned in through the open window and stared at Mo's mouth. Mo said, "Thrash, what are you doing?"

"Trying to find your enormous sweet tooth," Thrash said.

Mo looked at Robby, Dot, and Alex, and then they burst out laughing. Robby said, "Thrash, a 'sweet tooth' isn't an actual tooth. It's just an expression for people who love to eat sweets, like candy, cake, and ice cream."

Thrash frowned. "Well, how could I possibly know *that*? I was only born a few months ago, and . . . and Terrans don't even eat food!"

Reaching through the window, Alex put his hand on Thrash's shoulder and said, "I'm sorry, son. Please don't be upset. We weren't laughing at you."

"Really?" Thrash said.

"Yes, really!" Dot said. "We only laughed because you made us realize that 'sweet tooth' is a very silly expression!"

"Oh," Thrash said. "I guess I understand." He looked at the purple cake on the table. "Sometimes I wish I *could* eat food." Thrash turned and walked back toward the barn.

Both Robby and Mo wore Cyber-Sleeves that allowed them to share emotions with their Terran siblings. Mo held up her arm to display her glowing Cyber-Sleeve and said, "I don't need *this* to tell me Thrash is sad."

Robby looked at the cake and said, "And now I'm not hungry anymore. Mom, Dad, may Mo and I be excused?"

Dot nodded, and Alex smiled and said, "No worries. The cake will taste just as good tomorrow."

Mo and Robby went out the kitchen door. Twitch said, "C'mon, gang. I have an idea for cheering up Thrash!" She ran for the barn, and her siblings followed fast behind.

CHAPTER 2
STIRRING THE POT

Bumblebee was training in the driveway as Twitch, Hashtag, Nightshade, Jawbreaker, Mo, and Robby ran into the barn. They moved past bales of hay until they found a very sad-looking Thrash sitting on top of an old refrigerator.

Twitch said, "Stop looking so glum, Thrash. I know how we can be included at dinner. We'll learn how to cook!"

Thrash's eyes went wide. "That's a great idea!" he said. "If we help prepare meals, then we'll be part of special family time!"

Mo said, "I vote that we make cookies! Mom and Dad love cookies, and their anniversary is tomorrow! It's perfect timing!"

"Hang on," Robby said. "Not to be a downer, but . . . remember Mom's house rules, including 'No Bots in the House'? She made that rule to prevent accidental damage to the house and furniture, so the kitchen is definitely off limits."

Jawbreaker said, "What if we build our own kitchen?"

Everyone looked at Nightshade, who was a scientist and also very good at building things. Working in secret, Nightshade had transformed the Maltos' barn into the Dugout, a series of secret underground rooms and play areas for the Terrans. Nightshade said, "As much as I would enjoy the opportunity to construct a kitchen, safety concerns discourage the use of heating elements within barns that contain highly flammable contents, such as hay."

"Maybe we don't need heat," Robby said. "Isn't there such a thing as no-bake cookies?"

"I'll check!" Hashtag said. She extended her satellite dish, looked at her tablet's display, and rapidly searched dozens of websites. "Okay, I found a recipe for no-heat, no-bake chocolate chip cookies!"

Robby said, "What are the ingredients?"

"Let's see," Hashtag said. "We'll need butter, vanilla extract, brown sugar, milk, salt, oat flour, and chocolate chips."

Mo said, "I'm sure we have all that stuff. Dad keeps the kitchen cupboards filled with baking supplies and—"

At the sound of approaching footsteps, Mo stopped talking. Robby said, "Sounds like Mom and Dad are coming."

Twitch whispered, "Let's keep our cookie plans a secret so we can surprise them."

Alex and Dot entered the barn and found the kids. Looking at Thrash, Dot said, "Dad and I are so sorry that you and anyone else felt left out at dinnertime."

"Thanks," Thrash said. "I know you didn't mean to exclude anyone."

Alex said, "I'm sure if we put our heads together, we can come up with ideas for *everyone* to feel included at dinner."

"But let's save those ideas for now," Dot said. "Tomorrow is a school day. Robby and Mo have to do their homework, and the rest of you need to prepare for your class with Bumblebee in the morning."

The Terrans said good night to their parents and their siblings, Robby and Mo. Before Mo left the barn, she leaned close to Twitch and whispered, "Robby and I will bring the ingredients to you tomorrow, before we leave for school!"

"I'll tell the others," Twitch said. "We're gonna have so much fun!"

CHAPTER 3
MESSY MALTOS

"Hurry," Mo whispered, "before Mom and Dad come downstairs."

"I am hurrying!" Robby whispered back.

Mo and Robby were getting ready for school earlier than usual so they would have time to gather the cookie-making materials for the Terrans. Moving quickly and quietly in their kitchen, they placed the ingredients into a large metal baking pan that also held a mixing bowl, several spoons, and a measuring cup. Robby picked up the pan and said, "Oh! We still need milk and butter."

"I'm on it!" Mo said as Robby went out the door and headed for the barn. Mo grabbed a small carton of milk and a partially unwrapped stick of butter from the refrigerator and raced outside after Robby.

Following Robby into the barn, Mo didn't see her Terran siblings or Bumblebee. She assumed they were in the lower levels of the Dugout, but when a wide trapdoor flipped open in the floor in front of her, she was so surprised that she lost her grip on the butter stick and it went flying into a bale of hay.

Bumblebee poked his head up through the trapdoor's hatch. He saw Robby holding a pan loaded with various things and Mo holding a milk carton. "Good morning!" Bumblebee said. "What's going on?"

Thinking fast, Robby said, "We, um . . . had too much food in the kitchen refrigerator, so . . . we need to store some in the barn fridge."

"Oh," Bumblebee said as Robby carried the pan to the old refrigerator. "Need any help?"

"Thanks, but we're all set," Mo said as she picked up the butter stick, which now had numerous bits of hay stuck to it.

From outside the barn, Alex called out, "Robby and Mo, where are you? We need to leave now or you'll be late for school!"

"Be right there!" Robby shouted back.

He and Mo quickly shoved the pan and all of the ingredients into the refrigerator.

Just then Twitch's head popped up beside Bumblebee in the trapdoor hatch. Looking at Robby, Twitch said, "I heard shouting. Is everything all right?"

"Everything's fine," Robby said with a wink. "Mo and I had to put some *stuff* in the fridge here."

"Ah, some *stuff*," Twitch said knowingly. "See you after school!"

Robby and Mo ran past the hatch and out of the barn just in time to wave goodbye to Dot as she drove off in her park ranger truck. They were halfway to the family's minivan, where Alex was already seated behind the wheel, when Mo said, "Oh no! I meant to pull some messy bits of hay out of the butter I dropped, but I didn't have time. I wish I could have told Twitch!"

"Don't worry," Robby said. "I'm sure Twitch or one of the other Terrans will notice and clean up the butter."

"I hope you're right," Mo said. "I wouldn't want to eat chocolate chip and *hay* cookies!"

CHAPTER 4
A STICKY SITUATION

Shortly after Dot, Alex, Robby, and Mo left the farm, Bumblebee summoned the Terrans up from the Dugout and into the barn. Bumblebee said, "I'm afraid I'll have to postpone our class for today. I just received a message from Optimus Prime and Megatron. They need my help cleaning up a mudslide near a hiking path in Witwicky National Park. Can you take care of yourselves while I'm gone?"

"Sure, Bumblebee," Twitch said. "Don't worry about us!"

Bumblebee stepped out of the barn and into the driveway. The Terrans watched from the barn as Bumblebee leaped and somersaulted, shifting his body parts in midair to change into his yellow sports car alt mode. He landed on his tires and zoomed away, leaving a cloud of dust behind him.

"Now we can make cookies!" Twitch said. She went to the refrigerator and removed the baking pan and other items that Robby and Mo had delivered. Turning to Hashtag, she said, "You have the recipe. What do we do first?"

Hashtag consulted her tablet's display and said, "First, we melt two tablespoons of butter and a half cup of brown sugar in a bowl, and then we add three tablespoons of milk and one teaspoon of vanilla extract. Then we mix in the other stuff, form the dough into cookie shapes, and put them in the refrigerator for twenty minutes."

Looking at the butter stick, Thrash said, "Is butter supposed to have pieces of hay in it?"

"Let's find out," Hashtag said as she searched websites for data. "It says here that butter is made from the cream of cows' milk, and that cows eat hay, but . . . I don't think butter contains hay."

"Must be a special type of butter!" Jawbreaker said.

Thrash scooped the brown sugar and the butter with bits of hay into the mixing bowl. Nightshade said, "Without a stove, how shall we melt these ingredients?"

"With my lasers!" Twitch said. With a bright burst of light, Twitch changed into her drone mode and fired her lasers directly into the bowl. "I can get a better angle as a drone," she explained. The energy beams melted the ingredients but also cracked the bowl. "Oops!" Twitch said.

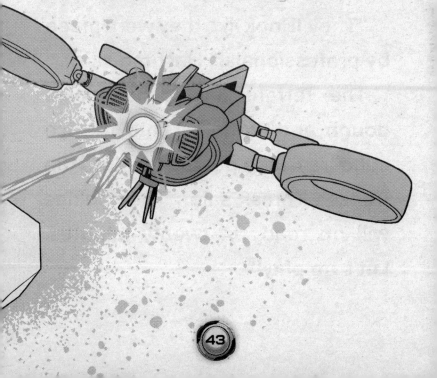

As Twitch changed back into her bot mode, Thrash opened the refrigerator and removed an ice cube tray. "Let's put the dough into this tray's little square compartments, and then our cookies will all come out the exact same size."

"They'll look like they were made by professionals!" Hashtag said.

The Terrans mixed the cookie dough and stuffed it into the ice cube tray, then put the tray into the freezer. Thrash said, "The cookies will be ready in twenty minutes. Let's go play!"

The Terrans ran out of the barn and into the nearby woods, where they played hide-and-seek and capture the flag. They had so much fun that they lost track of time.

Hours later, when they heard the family minivan and Dot's truck pulling into the driveway, Thrash said, "We forgot the cookies! We need to get to the barn . . . fast!"

CHAPTER 5
MALTO FAMILY MEAL

As Dot got out of her park ranger truck, and Alex, Robby, and Mo got out of the minivan, they saw the Terrans running into the barn. Alex said, "What's up with the Terrans? And where's Bumblebee?"

"I don't know what the kids are up to," Dot said, "but Bumblebee went to help Optimus Prime and Megatron clean up a mudslide."

Just then Bumblebee, in his sports car mode, zoomed into the driveway and came to a stop near Dot's truck. His yellow body was covered with mud and dirt. Changing into his bot mode, he said, "Pardon my appearance. I should have stopped at a car wash, but I wanted to get

back to the Terrans as soon as I could."

Mo and Robby felt their Cyber-Sleeves pulsate and glow. Frowning, Mo said, "The Terrans . . . they're all so sad right now."

Robby looked to the barn and said, "Here they come."

Twitch carried the ice cube tray filled with cookie dough as she led the Terrans out of the barn and over to Mo, Robby, Dot, Alex, and Bumblebee. Holding up the tray so everyone could see the frozen gobs of dough, Twitch said, "These were supposed to be cookies, but we left them in the freezer for too long, and now they're hard as rocks, and . . . I accidentally cracked a mixing bowl."

"Also," Hashtag said, "maybe we should have removed the hay from the butter?"

"Oh no," Mo said. "The hay in the butter was my fault!"

Alex laughed. "Don't worry about the bowl or the hay. I'm so proud of you all for even *trying* to make cookies!"

"We wanted to surprise you with cookies for your anniversary," Thrash explained. "And then we could be part of your dinner ritual, even though we don't eat."

"Oh, you darlings!" Dot said. "Dad and I said we were sorry for making you feel left out, but being sorry isn't enough. That's why we're making some changes around here." She turned to Bumblebee. "Bumblebee, in the back of my truck, I have a surprise. Could you please get it?"

Bumblebee went to the truck and removed a large folding metal picnic table. Dot said, "We can use this table outside in warm weather or inside the barn. Now everyone can join in at dinnertime."

All the Malto children cheered. Thrash said, "What a great surprise. Thank you, Mom!"

"I have a surprise too," Alex said. "Even though bots don't eat food, cooking can be lots of fun, especially when a family cooks together, so I decided we should collaborate on a book." He held up a notebook. On the notebook's cover, he'd written *Malto Family Cookbook*.

Nightshade said, "I anticipate many experiments with edible organic compounds."

Jawbreaker extended his arms and said, "I anticipate a family hug!"

Bumblebee looked at the mud on his own arms and said, "Maybe I should wash off first?"

"Too late!" Jawbreaker said as everyone moved in for a big hug.

Ready for another **TRANSFORMERS EARTHSPARK** adventure?

Here's a sneak peek of Book 3,

MAY THE BEST BOT WIN!

"Dad is home with Robby and Mo!" Hashtag said. "Let's greet them!" She ran out of the Malto family's barn, followed by Twitch, Thrash, Nightshade, Jawbreaker, and Bumblebee. The first Tranformers to be born on Earth, along with their trainer and friend, Bumblebee, came to a stop at the edge of the driveway, where they watched Alex, Robby, and Mo Malto climb out of their van.

Bumblebee said, "How was school today?"

Robby held up a small metal trophy. "Check out this award!" he said. "My cloned-cabbage-leaf experiment won the science fair!"